BABY WREN AND THE GREAT GIFT

For my friends at Laity Lodge, and
the Canyon Wrens who fill the air with singing.—SLJ

To my father, Charles Joseph Corace, who found his own song.—Jen

ZONDERKIDZ

Baby Wren and the Great Gift
Copyright © 2016 by Sally Lloyd-Jones
Illustrator copyright © 2016 by Jen Corace

Requests for information should be addressed to:
Zonderkidz, 3900 Sparks Ave SE, Grand Rapids, Michigan 49546

ISBN 978-0-310-73389-8

Design: Helen Capone

Printed in China

16 17 18 /DHC/ 11 10 9 8 7 6 5 4 3 2 1

BABY WREN AND THE GREAT GIFT

WRITTEN BY SALLY LLOYD-JONES

ILLUSTRATED BY JEN CORACE

In the narrow crevice
of a giant rock face
in a great wide canyon
a baby inside her tiny nest
peeped out.

The baby was little
and brown
and a wren.

And she watched in the air
from her nest in the sky.

And the world was filled with such wonderfulness.
Monarchs in the milkweed.
Breezes in the switch grass.
And a glittering river that ran on.

The baby hopped out
onto the ledge.

Just then, in a flash of blue . . .

a kingfisher dived down into the river, and came up and out with a fish.

"Oh!" said the tiny wren. "How wonderful!"

"Come fishing with me," the kingfisher said.

"But I can't dive," said the baby.

The kingfisher flew low over the water and away.

"Why aren't I a kingfisher?" wondered the baby.

"So I could fish, too?"

But no one answered.
Monarchs played in the milkweed.
A breeze rustled in the switch grass.
And the glittering river ran on.

The baby crept along the wall.

Just then, some ring-tailed cats scampered up the rock face.

They did cartwheels on their ring-tails.

"Oh!" said the tiny wren. "How wonderful!"

"Do cartwheels with us," they said.

"But I don't have a ring-tail," said the baby.

The ring-tailed cats cartwheeled together
up the rocky face, and away.

"Why aren't I a ring-tailed cat?"
the baby wondered.

"So I could do cartwheels, too?"

But no one answered.
Monarchs played in the milkweed.
A breeze rustled in the switch grass.
And the glittering river ran on.

Just then, some sunfish splashed around and around in the water.

"Oh!" said the tiny wren. "How wonderful!"

"Come and splash with us," they said.

"But I can't swim," said the baby.

The sunfish dropped back into the deep dark water.

"Why aren't I a sunfish?"
the baby wondered.

"So I could swim and splash, too?"

But no one answered.
Monarchs played in the milkweed.
A breeze rustled in the switch grass.
And the glittering river ran on.

Just then, the winds picked up
and a great storm blew into the canyon.
The baby hopped back to the ledge.
High above her, two eagles circled in the sky.

"Oh!" said the wren. "How wonderful!"

"Come and see the thunderclouds!" they said.

"But the storm is too big for me," said the baby.

The eagles soared higher and higher and away.

"Why aren't I a brave eagle?"
the baby wondered.

"So I could fly in the stormy sky?"

"What can I do that's wonderful?" she asked.

And, just then, the sun painted the whole canyon pink.

The tiny, fairy bird
sat very still and very quiet.
And looked.
And looked.
And looked.

And what she saw couldn't fit inside her
it bumped into her heart
it dazzled in her eyes
it pushed on her throat
until
the tiny trembling bird
with all her tiny might
sang
by herself
a song.

"For all of the sky
and shining sun,
for milkweed, monarchs,
and rivers that run,
for kingfishers,
sunfish, ring-tailed cats,
for eagles and thunderclouds
and storms blowing through—

and that I'm here too!

Thank you!"

And her bright carol reached
down to the river
and leaped off the cliff walls
and soared into the sky.

"You are only little," called the eagles.

"But your song is bigger than the whole canyon! How wonderful!"

And the kingfisher dived
and the ring-tailed cats climbed
and the sunfish splashed
and the eagles soared

and a little wren filled the air with singing.

And the glittering river ran on.